Vasalisa
and her Magic Doll

adapted and illustrated by
RITA GRAUER

Philomel Books ❧ New York

*For those who are willing to journey
out of darkness into the light.*

AUTHOR'S NOTE

Vasalisa and Her Magic Doll is derived from the Aleksandr Afanasev
version of the Russian folktale "Vasalisa the Beautiful" which appears in
the following collections: *Russian Fairy Tales* translated by Robert Chandler
(Shambhala/Random House, 1980); *Russian Fairy Tales* translated by
Norbert Guterman (Pantheon, 1945); *The Firebird and Other Russian
Tales* edited by Jacqueline Onassis and translated by Boris Zvorykin
(Studio Books/Viking Press, 1978); *Russian Folktales* translated by Marie
Ponsot (Golden Press, 1960). Interpretations beyond the original tale are
designed to illuminate the story's deeper significance and are drawn
from a variety of sources, including the interpretive work of Carl Jung,
Bruno Bettelheim, Marie-Louise von Franz, and Clarissa Pinkola Estés,
as well as other tales involving Vasalisa and Baba Yaga.

Copyright © 1994 by Rita Grauer. All rights reserved. This book, or parts thereof,
may not be reproduced in any form without permission in writing from the publisher.
Philomel Books, a division of The Putnam & Grosset Group, 200 Madison Avenue,
New York, NY 10016. Philomel Books, Reg. U.S. Pat. & Tm. Off. Published simultaneously
in Canada. Printed in Hong Kong by South China Printing Co. (1988), Ltd.
Book design by Gunta Alexander. The text is set in Berkeley Old Style.

Library of Congress Cataloging-in-Publication Data.
Grauer, Rita. Vasalisa and her magic doll / by Rita Grauer. p. cm.
Summary: A retelling of the old Russian fairy tale in which beautiful Vasalisa
uses the help of her doll to escape from the clutches of the witch Baba Yaga.
[1. Fairy tales. 2. Folklore—Soviet Union.] I. Title. PZ8.G748Vas 1994
398.21′0947—dc20   91-47513 CIP AC ISBN 0-399-21986-2
10 9 8 7 6 5 4 3 2 1 First Impression

A long, long time ago, at the edge of the deep, dark Russian forest, there once stood a tiny little village named Drov, where the sun shone only half the year, and the light in people's homes was a precious, precious thing. It was there a widow lived with her two daughters. The elder was Svetlana, and the younger, Vasalisa.

In all of Drov, there was no child more lovely than Vasalisa, and the villagers were drawn to her like moths to a flame.

"Oy!" they'd exclaim. "She looks just like a little doll." And they'd pinch her cheeks and pat her head and carry on so, that her sister became incurably jealous.

"Pretty Vasalisa. Pretty little kukla. You're no better than a doll!" she meanly teased. "Tiny kukla. Helpless kukla. You are easily broken!"

"There, there, little angel," the widow would comfort. "Svetlana doesn't really mean to hurt you." Her mother's love always dried Vasalisa's tears and made the sweet child feel much better.

But, as fate would have it, the widow grew ill and took to her bed. And one sad autumn day, knowing her end was near, she called each of her daughters to the bedside to give them a parting gift.

"I will leave to you our home and all within it," she told Svetlana, "if you will promise to care for Vasalisa until she is grown, and learn to love her with all of your heart."

"I will promise, Mama dear," Svetlana replied, full of good intentions.

To Vasalisa, the widow left something quite different. "It is a Magic Doll," she explained, "your very own kukla—she will never desert you. Love her well, but show her to no one. She will help you whenever you need it."

The poor child could not hold her tears back. Her mother held her tightly. "All will be well, my little one," she whispered, "if you simply do what lies before you." Then, with Vasalisa in her arms, the widow breathed one last sigh and fell into the sleep of endless peace.

For several weeks, as the days of fall grew darker, life was rather peaceful for the sisters—until one morning at the marketplace, when someone remarked that Vasalisa's hair had grown so long, it looked like flowing satin ribbons. Svetlana could hardly contain her jealousy and walked home alone.

"Okh!" thought Vasalisa. "I must do something quickly or Svetlana will be mean to me for certain." And she ran home to cut her hair short.

But the very next day, when the sisters were seen again, the villagers started making quite a fuss.

"Look at Vasalisa's new short hair!" one of them exclaimed, and all of the others gathered around. "Why, it shines like the night aglow with the moon."

"Okh!" thought Vasalisa. "Now what shall I do? Things are only getting worse!" She ran home to cover her hair so that no one would see it, but when she returned, the villagers fussed all the more.

"Vasalisa's babushka is *so* beautiful," they said. "She always looks *so* pretty!"

In no time at all, Svetlana was filled with jealous rage and she locked Vasalisa in the house.

There Vasalisa stayed, with only her doll for company. She served it tea and told it stories, and braided its woolen hair. When she grew sad, the Magic Doll said, "Your sister will love you again."

"But I make my sister so unhappy. How can you say that she will love me?" Big tears slid down Vasalisa's cheeks.

"I am made of a mother's love, and I often see the truth when others don't. Do not have regrets," said the doll. "Your sister will love you again." Then she sang a song to cheer Vasalisa, and before long, Vasalisa was singing too.

That evening as Svetlana approached the house, she heard the singing and rushed inside. "How can you sing?" she shouted, as Vasalisa slid the Magic Doll into her pocket. "You should be lonely and sad, all locked up within the house." And with that, she lunged toward her sister.

But Vasalisa moved quickly aside and Svetlana fell against the table. Over went the candle, and out went the precious, precious light.

For a moment, all was still and silent in the dusk of early evening.

"Now look what you've done…" Svetlana's voice was hushed and trembling. "You must go and get the light from Baba Yaga. If you don't, we will live in darkness forever." And she pushed Vasalisa out of the room.

Poor Vasalisa. You see, Baba Yaga was a terrible old crone who loved to dine on human flesh, and she lived at the heart of the deep, dark Russian forest in a house that walked on giant chicken legs. Yet if a flame went out in Drov, there was but one way to rekindle it, and that was with Baba Yaga's light.

Vasalisa lifted the doll out of her pocket. "Please, dear kukla," she pleaded, "you must tell me what to do. I promise I shall listen!"

"We shall seek the light together," the Magic Doll told her. "If you do what lies before you, then all will be well."

So, as the deep-red glow of twilight faded and the stars began to show themselves to the chilly Russian night, Vasalisa safely tucked the doll into her pocket and set out for Baba Yaga's woods.

The nighttime forest was vast and foreboding with its endless canopy of trees. "Beware Baba Yaga's woods!" the cedars murmured. "Beware the strangeness of the crone!" the birch trees moaned.

When at last the moon's face peered over the tops of the trees, Vasalisa could see a dark rider on a black horse. He was lingering in the distance beyond a bramble thicket.

"Follow me," he beckoned, his ebony stallion pawing at the ground.

Vasalisa wanted to turn and run toward home, but the Magic Doll encouraged her to stay, saying, "Do what lies before you, and all will be well."

So the fearful child gathered her cloak around her and struggled through
the brambles to meet the phantom guide. Twisted branches grasped at her as
she let herself be led into the night. The moon rose higher in the sky, casting
eerie shadows. The wind blew, and the shadows leapt like demons dancing.

"Do what lies before you..." Vasalisa told herself. "Do what lies before you..."

The horseman took her deep within the woods. When the edge of dawn came
creeping through the trees, he slipped into the shadows, where he vanished.

"Ah me, dear kukla," sighed Vasalisa. "The dark rider is gone, and without
him, I'm afraid we are lost."

Before the Magic Doll could say a word, the sound of galloping hooves announced the coming of another horseman. Vasalisa quickly turned her head, and out of the rays of the breaking dawn emerged an ivory-colored stallion, his rider clad in purest white.

She watched him gallop past like a sudden flash of light and enter a small clearing where an ordinary wooden izba stood. Over the little house he flew. Up, up, up, through an opening in the trees he went, and he merged into the brightness of the morning sun.

Then, the air crackled with the most horrible sound, and Vasalisa's eyes opened wide. The house had risen up upon a pair of chicken legs and was strutting around in circles.

"Fie, fie, Russian Bones!" screeched a voice from within the house. "Tell me why you have come here!"

Vasalisa said nothing—she was trembling too hard. But the Magic Doll encouraged her to speak, saying, "You know why you have come here. Do what you must do."

Heeding the doll's advice, the quivering child stepped out from behind a tree. "I have c-come for your light, Ba-Baba Yaga," she sputtered, for her teeth were chattering fiercely.

"Not so quickly," laughed the voice. "You must catch me first." And with that, the izba bolted from the clearing.

"Do not waste a moment, Vasalisa," urged the doll.

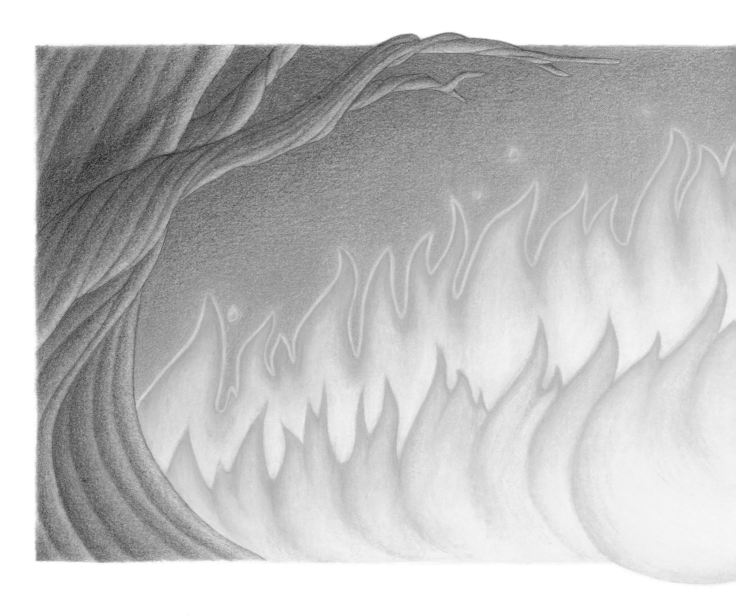

Over the biggest boulders, through the scratchiest thickets, and into the heart of the woods ran Vasalisa, following the wooden izba.

Even when a rain of smoky ashes started falling and the color crimson shimmered in the air, and even when the smell of something charred hung on the breezes and blackened limbs were everywhere, still she followed the izba.

But when at last they came upon a river with towering flames arising from its surface and a heat so thick it made it hard to breathe, why—Baba Yaga's wooden izba jumped right into the river of fire! Vasalisa watched in disbelief.

"Oh no!" she cried, and she fell down on her knees, weeping.

Through her tears, she noticed something prancing amid the flames—a horseman dressed in red, riding atop a fiery steed.

"Baba Yaga's wooden izba has passed safely through the fire. So shall you, Vasalisa, so shall you!" he called out.

Brushing the tears from her face, Vasalisa crawled to her feet and took a step toward the river of fire.

"So shall you, Vasalisa, so shall you," the fire hissed. Again she took a step toward the river.

"Do what lies before you, Vasalisa," encouraged the doll. And Vasalisa stepped *into* the blazing river!

No sooner had she entered the flames, than to her side sprang the horseman. He swept her into his arms, carried her safely through the blaze, then disappeared into the river once more.

There, in front of Vasalisa, sat the house of the dreaded Baba Yaga. It was surrounded by a fence of human bones, with skulls topping each of the posts. The gate was not a gate but spindly arms, and the latch was not a latch but teeth.

"Okh!" gasped Vasalisa, when out of the house a pair of hands came crawling like spiders. They unlocked the latch, then went back inside, leaving the door wide open.

Vasalisa swallowed hard. "Ba-Baba Yaga," she called. Not a sound came from the tiny izba. "I know why I have come here," she reminded herself, "and I know what I must do." And she tiptoed to the door to have a peek.

A lovely fire was burning in the hearth, and a table was set with a plate of bliny. The golden pancakes smelled so good that Vasalisa's stomach began to growl.

"Ba-Baba Yaga," she called again, but no one was in sight.

She was desperately hungry so she stepped through the door and hastily scurried to the table. "I hope Baba Yaga won't be too upset when she finds that we have eaten her bliny," she confided, sharing the luscious pancakes with her doll.

When the meal was finished, she leaned back in the chair, gazing at the fire's lovely light. "What a journey we have made, dear kukla," she sighed.

Then suddenly, the fire in the hearth grew so bright that Vasalisa had to shield her eyes. The flames began to wriggle like an old woman dancing, until in fact, they became just that. Out of the fire leapt Baba Yaga!

"Fie, fie, Russian Bones, do you think you shall have my light?" she screeched. "What have you brought me in return?"

"No-no-nothing. I have nothing!" the startled child replied. And she quickly hid the Magic Doll beneath her cloak.

"Well, perhaps I should eat you—the way you ate my bliny. I am quite hungry, you know." The old crone sneered, revealing her tarnished iron teeth. "But first I will take a nap, and then when I wake up, we shall see what we shall see."

Baba Yaga whistled and the spidery hands appeared, fetching a cooking pot filled with water. She took it from the hands and set it over the fire. Then she sat down on the chair, propping her pale and bony legs up on the table. The hands crawled up to rest on her shoulders, and instantly the old crone began to snore.

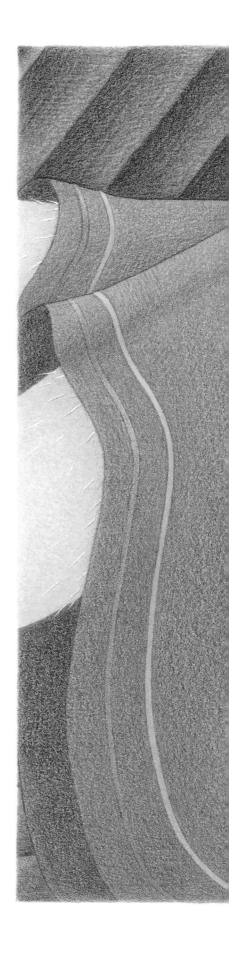

As she slept, her size seemed to change—her feet slammed the door shut and her nose poked a hole in the ceiling.

"Now what shall I do?" Vasalisa began to worry, as she nervously lifted the doll from under her cloak. "Baba Yaga is so big, she will eat me in one bite."

"Do what lies before you, Vasalisa," the Magic Doll encouraged. Her voice had grown so soft that Vasalisa could hardly hear her.

"What's the matter, dear kukla? What is happening to you?" she asked.

"The journey has made me tired, but it will be all right. Have faith. All will be well."

"I will have faith," she promised her little friend, "and I will do what lies before me."

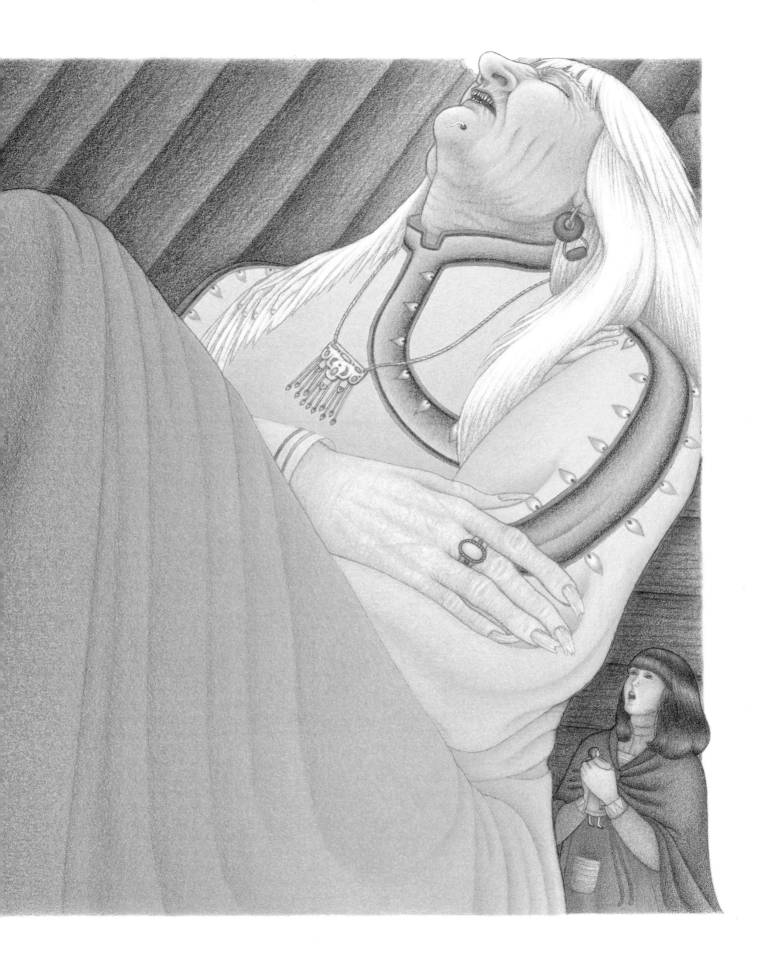

Then she tenderly placed the doll back in her pocket, and opened up the larder. She put meat, beets, cabbage, potatoes, carrots, onions, and vinegar into the pot to simmer, to make a borsch for the hungry old crone. Soon the air was filled with a scrumptious smell. "Mmmm..." Baba Yaga muttered in her sleep.

Vasalisa turned to look at her. Baba Yaga's nose seemed shorter.

After that, Vasalisa cleaned the bliny dish. She even swept and dusted. By the time she was done, the old crone's legs had fallen from the table and her feet just barely reached the floor.

The sun was setting and the silvery moon was rising, and the izba was getting rather chilly. So the brave young girl took a quilt down from the cupboard and covered the sleeping Baba Yaga.

"Why, she sleeps so soundly," Vasalisa realized. "She hardly scares me at all."

Then Vasalisa added some wood to the fire and sat down by the hearth with her doll. "What a long, long day this has been," she sighed, cradling the doll in her arms.

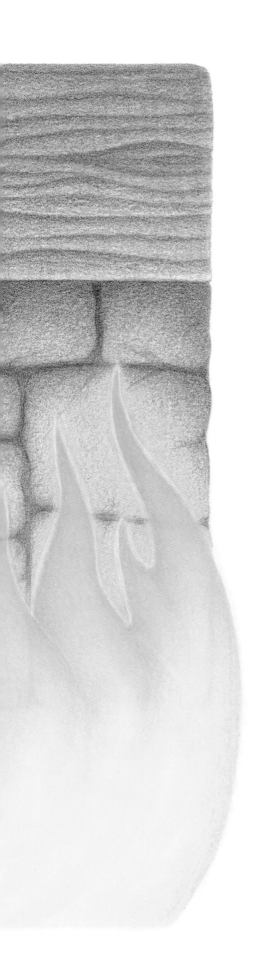

But her faithful little friend was silent. Not a sound or a move did she make. "Are you sleeping?" Vasalisa asked hopefully. And then she began to cry.

The sound of her crying caused the old crone to stir. She awakened and looked all around. "Fie, fie, Russian Bones! I see you do have something to give me—so perhaps I will not eat you after all. Perhaps I will give you my light," she bargained, "*if* you will give me that doll!"

"But she is made of my mother's love!" cried Vasalisa.

"She is only made of cloth and paint," laughed the crone. "And you are just as helpless as she is, if you cannot do what lies before you."

Vasalisa became as quiet as a windless lake. She lifted the doll's face to meet her own. A gentle smile was on the tiny mouth and a peaceful look was in its painted eyes.

She held it close for a very long time—until something began to stir within Vasalisa. A still, small voice began to speak within her heart, and she knew then what she must do.

Vasalisa kissed the Magic Doll goodbye and gave it to Baba Yaga forever.

The old crone was so pleased, she started dancing with the doll, while the spidery hands danced upon her shoulders. Then the table began to dance, and the cupboard and the chair—and the door and the windows flew open. Everything was dancing inside the wooden izba, and the izba was dancing too. Even the trees in the forest were dancing, along with the stars and the moon.

Into the fire Baba Yaga waltzed, and in a puff of smoke she was gone. "Take the light, Vasalisa," sang her voice from the flames. "And the light will carry you home!"

Never before had Vasalisa felt such joy. Her heart was filled with an unshakable happiness, as Baba Yaga's light lit her way back home through the deep, dark Russian forest.

When she stepped through the door with the candle, Svetlana ran to embrace her. "How happy I am to see you, little sister, and how worried I have been. From the moment you left, I was lonely and sad. I have *never* been as unhappy as I was without you."

Then she took Vasalisa's face in her hands, and with a voice as sweet as a songbird's, said, "Forgive me, sister dear, for treating you so unkindly—I love you as I love my very life."

And from that day on, as the candles burned brightly in the tiny little village of Drov, Vasalisa always listened to the voice within her heart, and all was truly well.